Cupig

The Valentine's Day Pig

By Claire Tattersfield

Illustrated by Rob Sayegh Jr.

FLAMINGO BOOKS

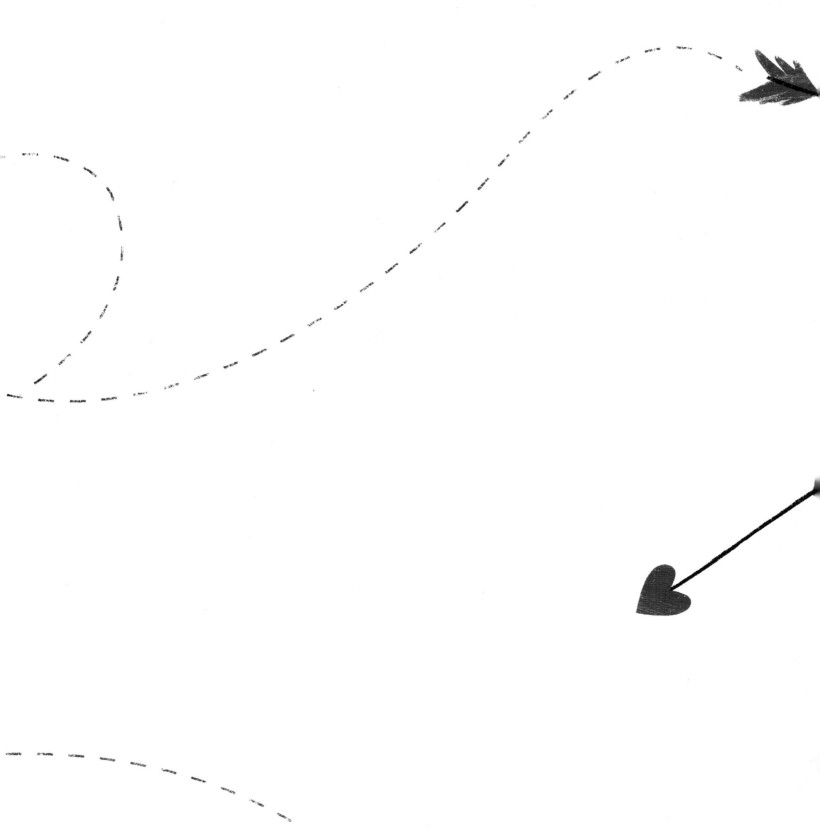

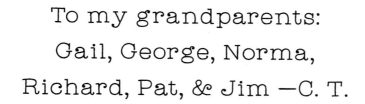

To my grandparents:
Gail, George, Norma,
Richard, Pat, & Jim —C. T.

For my forever valentine,
Meryl —R. S.

FLAMINGO BOOKS
An imprint of Penguin Random House LLC, New York

First published in the United States of America by Flamingo Books,
an imprint of Penguin Random House LLC, 2023

Text copyright © 2023 by Claire Tattersfield
Illustrations copyright © 2023 by Rob Sayegh Jr.

Visit us online at penguinrandomhouse.com.

Library of Congress Cataloging-in-Publication Data is available.

Manufactured in China

ISBN 9780593623107

1 3 5 7 9 10 8 6 4 2

TOPL

Design by Lucia Baez • Text set in Catalina Typewriter

The illustrations in this book were rendered using collage and digital painting techniques.

Cupig loved love.

She loved love more than butterflies
loved the sky above.

Every year on her favorite holiday

(which, coincidentally, was Valentine's Day),

she enjoyed spreading love and cheer

to every creature, far and near.

But when the weather got
rather iffy, aiming well
was rather tricky.

She may have stuck some arrows

in places she had not intended

and accidentally put arrows in hearts

that didn't need to be mended.

Cupig, the great lover of love,

may have made some mistakes.

Now Peanut Butter stopped loving Jelly
and fell in love with something smelly.
Anchovies have joined the picture
to make a most disgusting mixture.

It looks like Fork has just left Knife
even though they had a perfect life!
But now that Fork loves Knife no more,
they've moved into a different drawer.

Not to worry! Cupig thought.

Maybe these new romances

deserve a shot.

Remember how butterflies loved the sky above?
Well, Cupig may have compromised their love
when a gust of wind threw her arrow off course
and the butterfly fell for a horse.

Fly away
with me!

Salt and Pepper always got along fine.

Together they made any meal divine.

But when a stray arrow changed direction,

Pepper was no longer the object of Salt's affection.

Cupig kept on despite the wind and spray,
for what else could she do on Valentine's Day?

Needle and Thread had been a great team;
now they're falling apart at the seams.
Poor Thread just wants Needle back
since Needle left her for a haystack.

Dog and Bone are in a fight.

Now Dog won't even take a bite

of what was once her favorite bone

since Dog fell for a xylophone?!?

Paper has always loved Pen so,

    but Pen was forced to let him go

when Paper made the most unusual pair

    and fell in love with a polar bear!

This storm may have caused a mess,
Cupig thoughtfully assessed.

Now Cupig knew she'd miscalculated

and made these pairs discombobulated.

With the sky now clear, Cupig saw what she'd done.

This Valentine's Day, she knew love had not won.

Things hadn't exactly gone as expected,
and so Cupig sat back and reflected.

You can't eat spaghetti with-
out a fork and a knife!
You could try with a whisk,
but it wouldn't be right.

Needle and Thread just
can't be apart!
For who would adorn
my undies with a
heart?

Never before have I seen such a sorry sight.

I know in my heart I must make things right.

So she flew off again to fix her mistakes,

hoping she was not too late.

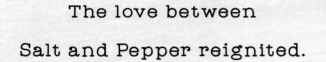

At last! Fork and
Knife have reunited.

The love between
Salt and Pepper reignited.

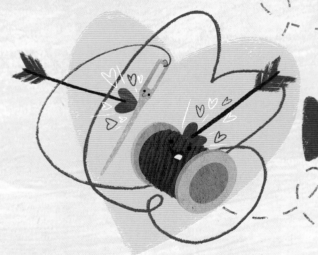

Needle and Thread's
love got a mend,

and Dog and Bone
were together again.

Paper and Pen were together once more, the love between them stronger than before.

Peanut Butter was back to loving Jelly the most.

(We can all agree Peanut Butter and Anchovies were *really, really gross.*)

Cupig really, really loved love,
just as butterflies again loved
the sky above.
And so she stowed her arrows away
until the next Valentine's Day.

Cupig, thinking of her recent missteps,
had no choice but to accept . . .

Sometimes she should just take a day off.

The end